TERRY DEARY

Stone Age Tales

The Great Storm

Illustrated by
Tambe

BLOOMSBURY EDUCATION
AN IMPRINT OF BLOOMSBURY

LONDON OXFORD NEW YORK NEW DELHI SYDNEY

Contents

White Bird · 7

Empty Tank · 14

Grey Stones · 20

Silver Moon · 28

Dangerous Plan · 34

Secret Search · 40

Wild Hills · 47

Fallen Hood · 52

Fact File · 60

You Try · 63

1

White Bird

Skara Brae, Orkney, Scotland – 5,000 years ago

The great white seabird soared over the shores of the island, searching for food. The grey sea was whipped into white waves by a sharp wind from the Arctic ice-fields. The only sound it could hear was the soft whisper of the wind in its feathers as it turned in sweeping circles.

It hung on the wind over a half-buried village of stone huts. Humans hurried along the lanes around them, bent and huddled against the cold wind off the sea. The bird closed its wide wings a little and dropped towards the sea.

Among the wave crests the dark sea showed no sign of the shoals of fish that lived below. But there were two dead fish scattered over the silver sands on the shore. All the gull had to do was land and fill its curving, yellow beak.

But it was an old bird. A wise bird. Between the rocks were lumpen shapes hidden under the skins of seals. They were humans, shivering in the shelter of the weed-slimed rocks. They were waiting for some greedy bird to land and snap at the fish. Then the humans would pull ropes and lift a net and snare the bird. It would make fine fresh meat for their cooking pot.

The gull swooped low and fast across the sand. It dipped its beak and snatched at a fish without landing.

In that moment it looked across the sands towards one of the faces under the sealskin cloaks. It was a girl human with a flame of red hair. In that glimpse the bird saw the girl's face flash with rage as she was robbed of her supper.

If a gull could laugh, then it would have jeered at her. Then the other human – a boy – snatched a pebble from the beach. He threw it straight and true at the gull. It caught the wing-tip of the bird. The gull gave a rasping cry of 'cark', and that made it drop the fish back onto the sand that hid the net. It climbed upwards towards the sea-grey clouds and looked back. The girl was on her feet, shaking her fist and laughing and shouting.

If the bird spoke human it would have known she was calling out, 'Serves you right you thieving, ugly bird! I hope you dive for fish and smash your greedy beak against a rock!'

The bird rode off on the wings of the wind to find safer food to fish for.

A boy with hair the colour of wet sand stood alongside the girl. 'It didn't work, Storm,' he sighed. 'I said it wouldn't. I catch more gulls with my stones. No one throws as well as I do.'

Her pale face turned red as her hair. She copied his voice with an added whine. 'Urr, Storm, I said it wouldn't work. Urr, aren't I the clever boy? No one throws as well as I do.' Her voice turned as fierce as her name. 'We eat nothing but fish. More fish. And then, just for a change, we have fish again. At least I am trying to catch birds for a bit of red meat. What are you doing?'

The boy shrank small inside his sealskin jacket. 'Nothing, Storm,' he muttered. 'It's just that we spent all morning catching those fish to bait the birds.'

The girl gave a wide grin. 'Exactly, Tuk.

So, we may not have a bird to eat, but at least we have a couple of fat herring.'

The boy frowned. 'One of them's been a bit chewed around by that white bird,' he said.

Storm nodded. 'Such a pity. That one was yours.'

His mouth fell open in dismay. 'But...'

'Never mind,' Storm went on quickly. 'Maybe Mother has a little old, stinking fish stew left over for you. And, if you are a really good little brother, I'll let you watch me eat my big, fat, fresh fish.'

She picked up her herring and led the way back to the village. But when they arrived there would be very little fish stew for Tuk.

2

Empty Tank

Storm ran into the covered passages that kept the whipping winds out of the stone houses. They usually had to squeeze past the villagers who moved from house to house or over to the main hall. Today the passageways were quiet and empty.

Storm ran through the stone door to her house. It stood open. She cried, 'Mother, I almost caught a huge gull...'

The main room of the house was empty. The fire was dying in the hearth in the middle and smoke drifted through the room.

'She's not here,' Tuk panted as he followed

her in. 'Father went out to the hills gathering peat. But Mother hardly leaves the house.'

The pottery dishes were neatly stacked on the stone dresser and the stone beds had their fur covers tidy. Mother's sewing had been dropped untidily, so she had left suddenly.

'Maybe that great white bird swooped down and snatched everyone up,' the girl gasped.

Tuk rolled his eyes to the ceiling. 'Storm, that's just a story that mothers tell their children. It stops the young ones straying too far from home.'

'No,' his sister argued. 'There really are huge birds with wings as wide as a man is tall. They could easily pick up a person. '

The boy sighed. 'But they couldn't pick up a whole village,' he told her. 'There's no one around.'

Storm stuck out a stubborn lip. 'Maybe there was a flock of them,' she said.

'And maybe a sea monster sneaked past us on the shore, swallowed everybody and then sneaked back into the sea.'

Storm's eyes were wide. 'I've heard of sea monsters too,' Storm said. 'Do you think that's what happened?'

'No,' Tuk said fiercely. 'I think we'll find

everyone in the great hall if we go along and look.'

Storm looked disappointed. 'I suppose so,' she said. She laid her fish down beside the hearth and wiped her hands on her fur trousers. 'Let's go and see.'

The passageways were dark but they knew their way. Soon they heard voices from a house that was larger than the rest. The village chieftain, Tane, was speaking. 'What should we do with a thief?' he roared.

'Throw him off the cliffs at Thule!' a woman cried back.

'Tie him with ropes to a rock and let the tide come in and drown him,' an old man croaked.

'That's too good for him,' a younger

man said. 'He should be made to fish every day until our stores are full again.'

'Aye,' the shouting woman called, 'make him feed us and then throw him off the cliffs!'

Most of the villagers mumbled that they agreed. But one woman turned and ran from the gloomy, lamp-lit hall. She pushed through the crowd of fifty villagers and stumbled out of the door.

'Mother?' Storm cried and ran after her. 'What's happened?'

Their mother kept walking but spoke over her shoulder in a broken voice. 'There has been a theft. Half of our winter fish supplies have gone. Someone has stolen them.'

'And you're upset because you think we'll starve?' Tuk asked.

The woman stopped and rubbed her red eyes. 'No, I'm upset because they say the thief is your father. They want revenge.'

19

3

Grey Stones

The early winter storms had left the village short of fish. In the summer the store of smoked fish had been full. But raging gales had made fishing impossible for the last two weeks. No one could remember such a storm. Egg-hunters like Tuk had not been able to climb down the cliffs to find gulls' nests to rob.

Everyone was getting short of food. One of the women had gone to the stone storehouse to get some herring and found it was half empty.

The village chieftain, Tane, was still

speaking. He was a large man with a deep voice. 'No one would want fish from Skara Brae except the people from the other side of the island,' Tane was saying angrily. 'Someone from our village must have given it to them.' The villagers' voices rumbled and agreed.

Storm turned and went back into the hall. 'The Far-Islanders love our fish,' she argued. 'They could have stolen it themselves.'

Tane's mouth was soft like seal blubber and it turned down in a sneer. 'The Far-Islanders are our friends. They trade the meat of their sheep for our fish. How dare you call our friends thieves?'

The girl's face turned red as her hair. 'How dare you call my father a thief, you walrus-faced sack of fish-guts with all the sense of a rock on the beach?'

The room fell silent as the villagers waited for Tane to burst with anger. Instead he gave a soft smile and spoke quietly.

'You are well named, Storm,' he said. 'You have a stormy temper.'

'I was named because I was born in a storm,' she snapped.

Tane took two steps towards her. 'No one goes far from the village,' he said, 'except your father, Orc.'

'He cuts peat in the wild hills for everyone to burn on their fires,' Storm argued. 'He can't do that on the beach.'

'No, he goes to the circle of stones,' Tane said, still soft. 'That is halfway between Skara Brae and Far-Island. He robs the fish store and uses his peat sledge to carry the fish to the Grey Stones. He meets the Far-Islanders and gives them the fish.'

Storm shook her head. 'Why would he do that?'

Tane snorted and spread his arms wide. 'The Far-Islanders would give him a sheep in return for the fish, so you and your

23

family can get through the winter with red meat.'

There were grumbles from the villagers in the hall. 'We should cut Orc to pieces and use his flesh for fish-bait,' the old man whined.

Storm shouted over the angry, muttering crowd. 'My father isn't a thief and we don't have any sheep meat in the house.'

A voice spoke gruffly behind her. 'Then what is this?'

Everyone turned towards the door. Tane's wife, Mara, stood there. She was as large as her husband. In her heavy hand she held up a leg from a skinned sheep. 'I found

this in Orc's living room,' she said. 'It was hidden under his bed.'

The villagers howled with rage. 'What a traitor! He wants to see us starve while he feasts.'

Tane raised his voice. 'He doesn't know we've discovered his theft. He'll come home and we'll catch him.'

An old man cried, 'That leg of lamb should go to the villager who catches Orc!'

'Yes,' the crowd cheered.

'No,' Tane's wife tried to argue. 'I found it... Tane and I should keep it.'

No one was listening.

Storm looked at her brother. 'We have to warn Father,' she said and dragged her brother out of the village into the freezing wind. The sun was setting behind the steep hill in the middle of the island. On top of the hill was a ring of stones, a long walk away.

Tuk pulled his sealskin coat tight around him and set off after his sister. 'Did you really call Tane a walrus-faced sack of fish-guts with all the sense of a rock on the beach?'

Storm nodded and made a sad face. 'I did. Do you think I was being too kind to him?'

'Far too kind,' Tuk said and laughed as he hurried over the frozen ground.

4

Silver Moon

Most days at Skara Brae were spent in work to help the villagers stay alive. But earlier in the year, on a summer day, Orc had taken Storm and Tuk on a journey to the stones. The food stores were full and the breeze was warm, and Orc had taken his children to the grey stones.

They had seen them from Skara Brae but Storm had fallen silent when they'd come close. The stones were three times as tall as Orc and stood in a circle a hundred paces wide.

'Who put them here?' Tuk had asked.

'Our grandfathers' grandfathers,' Orc had

said. 'They dragged them here on sledges like my peat sledge.'

'All that wood to make the sledges,' Storm had gasped. Wood was the most precious thing on the islands. Rare and too precious to burn when it was washed up on the shores. The villagers used the peat moss that Orc dug to give them heat for cooking.

After they had eaten a little fish Orc had scooped a hollow in the soil beneath the greatest stone. 'Put some of your fish there as a gift to the gods. They will make sure we catch plenty of fish.'

Storm had done as Orc told her.

Now that winter had come, and her father was called a thief, she followed the path to the stones and grumbled, 'Our gift of fish didn't work. That storm went on so long this year.'

'Maybe the gods were arguing with one another. The god of the sea might have had a row with the winds,' Tuk explained. The path led them up the coast with the sea to their left. It looked calm enough now and as blue-grey as the stones ahead of them.

'I hope the god of the sea won,' Storm sighed.

They heard their father working before they saw him. His spade was clanking as it struck the frosted earth. Squares of peat were stacked on the ground ready to load onto the

sledge. 'He needs the sledge for shelter when he stays out all night,' Storm explained to Tuk.

'I know that,' her brother said, sulkily. 'I'm not Tane – I have more sense than a rock on the beach.'

Orc looked up from his work and smiled. 'Just in time to help me load the peat,' he said. 'I'll get back to Skara Brae before sunset.'

Storm shook her head. 'You can't go back,' the girl said.

'They'll kill you,' Tuk added.

The smile slid from Orc's face like a seal off a rock. 'What's happened?' he asked.

Storm told the story of the theft and how the chieftain's wife had found a leg of sheep meat in the cupboard in their house. 'You didn't steal the fish, did you?' she asked her father.

Orc asked her questions.

Where had their mother been when Tane's wife, Mara, walked into the hall with the meat? Standing at the door to the hall.

What happened to the meat? The old man said it should go to the person who captured Orc.

What did Tane's wife think about that? She was angry.

Where was the rest of the dead sheep? Storm didn't know... but she was sure it wasn't in her home.

'So, who stole the fish and traded it for the sheep meat, Storm?'

The girl shrugged. 'I don't know.'

'What will they do next, Tuk?' the man asked.

'I don't know.'

Orc looked out over the green-grey sea. The sun was setting in an orange blaze to the west. The moon was rising in the east and slowly turning the frosted land from gold to silver.

The man spoke quietly. 'I know who stole the fish.' His eyes shifted back towards Skara

Brae. 'And I could guess what they will do next. I just didn't expect them to do it so soon.'

Storm looked back to where her father was staring. Her eyes were sharp as any sea eagle's. In the pale light she saw a dark shape leaving the half-hidden village of Skara Brae. It was dragging a sledge loaded with leather sacks. The sort of sacks that the villagers used to store their smoked fish.

The figure was heading their way.

'Hide,' Orc said.

5
Dangerous Plan

The path to the Far-Island village ran along the cliff top. Orc dragged the empty sledge to the stones at the other side of the circle.

Storm and Tuk each chose a stone to hide behind. A snowy owl hooted and hunted some mouse. Storm felt like the mouse as the dark figure climbed up from the village.

The girl shivered and waited. She risked a glance from her hiding place. The stranger had stopped and was looking at the pile of peat that Orc had left ready to load. She couldn't see the face under the fur hood, but

she felt its eyes were looking straight at her. Straight through her.

At last it hitched the rope over a stout shoulder and plodded on. When the figure was well down the path to the Far-Island Village Orc stepped out. 'Now, Storm, I need your help.'

'Anything,' she said, breathless.

'It sounds as if the villagers are furious with me. If I return to Skara Brae they'll kill me,' her father said.

'Tell them you didn't do it,' Tuk said.

'That's not good enough. I'll have to show them all who did do it. We need to find the rest of that sheep meat,' Orc went on.

'It will be in someone's cupboard... or hidden under their bed,' Storm said. 'You stay safe. I'll go in. I can easily find it. All the houses are built the same.'

Orc looked worried. 'It will be dangerous. The houses are so small. The thief may see you as soon as you go into their house. That's why we need Tuk.'

The boy grinned, his teeth sparkling in the moonlight. 'What we need is for someone to get the thief out of their house so you can slip in.'

His father nodded. 'How can you do that?'

'Easy,' the boy laughed. 'I'll run through the streets shouting for Storm. I'll cry out that our father is on his way back to Skara Brae with his peat sledge. Oh, I'll cry. Poor Father doesn't know the villagers are waiting to capture him!

And if they do they'll throw him over the cliff!
Oh, Storm, I'll shout, help me run to him!'

Orc nodded. 'Everyone in the village will
rush out. The first one to catch me will get
a feast of sheep-meat, remember.'

'The villagers are like fish,' Storm nodded.
'And you are the bait.'

'No one can run faster than me, Storm. If
they try to chase me then I'll be safe.'

She nodded. 'You can fly like the great
white bird.'

Her father said, 'If I run too fast they'll give up and go home. I'll have to stumble and slip a little. I'll have to let them get close enough to give them hope.'

'I suppose so,' she sighed. 'It will be dangerous.'

'Time to set off,' her father said. 'Help me load the peat onto my sledge and we'll drag it down to Skara Brae. I'll leave it in front of the main passage into the village. Tuk will run through the passages, and the villagers will all come looking for me near the sled.'

Storm said, 'I'll slip around to the back and search the thief's house.'

The northern winter night was long and the sun was a long time in rising. The sledge was loaded and the family made the slow journey back to Skara Brae, dragging the creaking wooden carrier behind them.

Orc looked ahead to see if anyone was on guard outside the village. His bright

eyes were looking for any movement, for any danger.

Storm and Tuk fell silent as they slowly helped their father drag the sled. Not one of them saw any danger ahead. There wasn't any.

They should have looked over their shoulders. Coming down the hill, a thousand steps behind them, was a large, dark figure pulling a lighter sledge with leather bags on the back.

Not even a snowy owl's eyes could have made out the face in the shadow of the hood. But it could have seen two eyes shining in the moonlight.

6

Secret Search

The family stopped the sledge a hundred paces from the front of the village. The hidden sun was turning the sky the colour of amber. Bright as the amber stones that Storm would sometimes find on the beaches.

They went over their plan again, as the wind carried away the sound of the other sledge that passed behind a frosted hill, and hid near the back of the village. The large, hooded figure waited and chewed on a piece of dried seal meat. The fierce eyes didn't blink.

Tuk walked down to the top of the slope that led into the half-buried village. Storm ran around to the back door. When she was ready she gave the cry of a snowy owl. Tuk breathed in the icy air and let out a wail as he ran down the slope into the dark passages.

'Storm... Mother... Orc is back... they'll hurt him... Storm... run and warn him!' he cried. His voice was an echo on the cold-hard, stone-hard, rough-cut walls of the houses. The echoes faded. For a long while there was silence.

Then there was a sleepy grumbling from inside those walls. Sleepy villagers woke slowly to hear Tuk's cries. What was he saying? Orc was back? There is a reward for catching Orc. Get up. Forget the cold. Stagger through the dark bedroom to find a coat, a cloak, a shawl, some boots, and stumble out into the street.

'He's at the front door,' someone cried.

The blubbery face of Chieftain Tane loomed like a yellow moon in the half-light. 'The leg of lamb goes to the first villager to lay hands on Orc,' he said. Villagers crashed and barged against the walls as they struggled out of the village and into the yellow sun in a green and gold sky.

Tane used his elbows to get to the front. 'There he is!' He set off to lumber over the frozen ruts in the earth but felt a sharp tug on his cloak as a young man pulled him back. 'I'll get him and claim the prize,' he said, laughing wildly.

Tane's foot slipped and he fell to the ground. He was gripping the wrist of the young man to tear himself free. They both fell in a tangle on the ground and rolled back down the slope as the greedy villagers trampled over them to get to Orc.

Even the old man got ahead of Tane in the scramble. Orc watched in wonder as the rabble roared towards him, slithering and squealing, battling, barging and blundering their way over the frozen path. Their fingers were like the claws of hunting owls, their eyes bright as codfish.

Orc waited until they were ten paces away and turned and trotted steadily away from the shelter of the peat sled. Behind the crowd Tuk laughed.

At the other side of the village Storm slipped into the empty streets. Every villager was out chasing her father. Even her mother had followed the villagers outside to watch.

Storm knew which house the thief lived in. She crept through the door. A lamp burned to show her the way.

There was a cupboard by the bed. She opened it to look for meat but it was full of winter furs and boots. Under the bed there were fishing rods and lines. The villagers would give up soon and be returning. Storm looked around wildly.

The only place she hadn't looked was in a stone chest in the corner. The lid was heavy but the girl struggled and slid it to one side. She smelled the smoked meat and then her

eyes grew used to the dark she could make out pieces of lamb. They had been carved into small pieces so each piece could make a fine meal for two people.

She grabbed the top piece and slipped it under her coat. She could show it to the villagers. She crept back towards the door and stepped outside into the still street.

She looked towards the front of the village.

If she had looked back she would have seen the large, hooded figure. She would have seen the frozen leg of lamb the figure held in the air, ready to come down and crack her skull.

But Storm was looking the wrong way.

7
Wild Hills

Storm heard a scream of pain and rage. She swung around and saw the figure in the hooded cloak was standing behind her, a frozen leg of lamb in its hand, ready to crash down. Suddenly, the sheep-meat fell and the hooded figure clutched at the hand that had been holding it.

Storm's bother Tuk stood, pale-faced and angry, behind. He had another stone ready to throw. 'You miserable little seal-pup, you broke my hand with your stone,' the figure raged.

'You would have done much worse to my sister,' Tuk said quietly. 'No one throws as well as I do. The next stone will be at your knee.'

For once Storm had no words. Her mouth hung a little open and at last she said, 'You saved me, Tuk.'

'We saved our father,' Tuk said. 'This is the fish thief, and that is more of the sheep meat they traded to stuff their fat faces. Now let's tell the village that our father is no robber.' He held the stone high and jerked it towards the hooded thief. 'Let's go and tell the village,' he went on.

Storm picked up the leg of sheep meat. She followed the thief through the low covered passages towards the slope at the front where all the villagers were gathered. Tuk spoke to her quickly. 'I woke the village and set them off after Father. Then I came around to see how you were getting on. I saw this hooded figure follow you.'

The villagers had given up the chase. Orc stood on a low hill a hundred paces from Skara Brae and looked back at the raging mob of people. People he'd thought were his friends.

Tane was shouting at the crowd. 'We must put a guard on the village; never let that wicked man return. Let him starve in the wild hills.'

'He'll probably go to see his Far-Island friends,' someone sneered, bitter and angry.

'We should take our fishing spears and drive the Far-Islanders away!' a woman cried. The crowd cheered and Tane waved a spear over his head.

'No,' came the sharp voice of Storm. She walked into the centre of the circle and held up the leg of sheep-meat. 'My father is no thief. I know the real thief.'

Tane stepped forward and pointed at the girl. 'See? She has some of her father's meat in her hand. We should throw the whole family out into the wild hills to freeze and die.'

But the crowd had fallen silent. Storm was standing quiet and half-smiling. 'I am no thief. My father is no thief. But I have found out who the thief is. This is the sheep-meat they have just brought back from the Far-Island. Their sled is full of the meat and it's at the far doorway.'

Tane's eyes bulged and his face turned red. 'Yes, that will be your father's sled. You probably helped him bring it back.' The chieftain swung around, 'See? The whole family have robbed their own friends. They all need to die in the cold.'

'What do you say to that?' the old man asked, pointing a twisted finger at her.

Storm gave a wide smile. 'I say you can search our house and find no meat. You can search the thief's house and find a stone box full of meat.'

Tane looked around, wild and fierce. 'You just put it there. Took it from your house and put it in the house of some poor helpless family while we were all out here.'

Storm shook her head slowly. 'I have the thief's helper here,' she said, pointing back to the entrance slope where the hooded figure stood. 'Blood on their hands.'

Everyone turned to where Tuk stood behind the hooded thief. Tuk reached up and pulled back the hood.

8
Fallen Hood

The hood fell from a furious face. The people of Skara Brae gasped. The face that looked out was the face of their chieftain's wife, Mara.

'Ah!' Tane roared. 'This is nonsense. All nonsense. Tell them, Mara – tell our dear friends why our chest is full of sheep meat.'

Mara glared. Her bottom lip stuck out. At last she muttered, 'We were looking after it for the people of Skara. I found a dead sheep in the wild hills and brought it back. It must have strayed from Far-Island and died of the cold.'

'Yes,' Tane said with a hearty, false laugh. 'We knew we'd be short of fish after the winter storms. We decided to keep it in our cold chest so we could feed everyone when the fish ran out.'

'Very good of you,' Storm said. 'So, who emptied our fish store?'

'Well... well, your father, of course,' Tane said, spreading his hands. 'The leg of sheep-meat was found under your bed.'

'Liar,' Storm's mother hissed. 'Your wife Mara said she found it there. She didn't. She used some of the meat you'd stolen. But you are greedy. You wanted more. We watched Mara heading to Far-Island last night for more meat. The sled was loaded with fish. She traded it. The meat is on her sled now.'

'Look in the fish store now,' Tuk said. 'It must be empty. Mara and Tane stole it all to feed their walrus-faced sack-of-fish-gut faces. Look in the store.'

The young man raced down the slope to look. He was soon back. 'It's empty,' he told the villagers.

'We should cut Tane and Mara to pieces and use their flesh for fish-bait,' the old man said.

'Send them to the wild hills!' a woman shouted.

'No,' came a firm voice from behind the villagers. Orc stood there. While they had been talking he had come down from the hill, silent as a fish.

'We need someone to spend long, cold hours fishing through the winter. Fishing so we can stay alive until spring returns.'

'Tane should do the fishing,' the old man croaked.

The villagers cheered at the idea. Storm stepped forward. 'So, walrus-faced sack of fish-guts, what do you choose? The wild hills or a winter by the freezing sea, fishing to feed us all?'

Tane looked across at Mara, his blubber lips turned down in hate. 'It was your idea,' he said. 'Never happy with what you had. Always wanting more food. You can help me do the fishing,' he snarled.

Mara stayed silent, but walked away to gather the fishing lines and nets.

The old man said, 'We can't have a thief for a chieftain.' The crowd murmured that he was right. 'We need someone brave and wise and strong.'

'You do,' Storm said. 'But I'm too young. Maybe a in a few years...'

'Not you, pebble-brain,' Tuk said. 'They mean our father.'

Storm sniffed. 'Well, yes, I was going to say he'd be best... or second best.'

And so it was that Orc became chieftain of Skara Brae. The villagers lived through the worst winter storms the island had ever seen.

The houses, half hidden in the earth, kept them warm. Tane and Mara kept them fed with fish.

When spring came Tuk and Storm climbed the cliffs to steal the eggs of gulls. The villagers caught seals while Chieftain Orc crossed the island to trade the soft skins for sheep meat. Summer brought the warm winds and content to Skara Brae... although not to weary and worn Tane and Mara.

And on those warm winds there soared a large white bird. He looked down on the

children climbing cliffs and setting traps to catch careless animals and birds.

Those human creatures were dangerous, the bird decided. Dangerous to any living thing. But, most of all, dangerous to one another.

The white bird sailed off to find the colder lands the humans hadn't conquered. Not yet.

FACT FILE

- Skara Brae, in Orkney, Scotland, was a small settlement where humans lived between 5,200 and 4,200 years ago. Eight houses have been found there, linked by low, covered passages.

- An ancient road crosses the island from Skara Brae. It passes near the Standing Stones of Stenness, a mysterious circle of massive slabs of rock.

- The houses were sunk into mounds that sheltered them through Orkney's harsh winters. Each house had a large, square room, with a stone hearth in the middle for heating and cooking. There were maybe fifty people living in Skara Brae at any one time.

- Each house had a low doorway with a stone-slab door that could be closed. The houses also have several stone-built pieces of furniture inside them – cupboards, seats and storage boxes. It's rare that everyday objects like these survive for us to see, as most furniture at the time was made of wood and rotted away hundreds of years ago.

• Drains were built under the village and each house had a simple toilet.

• Wheat and barley crops were grown in the fields.

• Fish bones and shells have been found in rubbish tips, so we know that the people of Skara Brae ate seafood. Bones found in the rubbish piles show that cattle and sheep were eaten as well, and red deer and wild boar were hunted. Villagers would have collected seabirds' eggs and trapped the birds for food, too. Bones of whales, walrus and killer whales show us what they feasted on when a big sea creature was washed ashore.

• The houses contain stone boxes in which limpet shells were found. They may have been filled with seawater to keep the shellfish alive. The limpets could then be eaten fresh, or used for fish bait.

• The inside of a Skara Brae house would have been dark and smoky. Fish would be hung from beams and the smoke would stop them rotting until the villagers were ready to eat them.

• What did they do on the long northern nights? Games and crafts seem to have been popular: dice, tools, beads, necklaces and brooches have been found.

YOU TRY

PARTY PLANNER

If you were Storm or Tuk, what would you have to eat at your birthday party? On a piece of paper, make a birthday invitation for a friend. You have to say where and when the party will happen – but you also have to tell them what food they will get at the party. Of course you can only offer the food that was around in Skara Brae 4,000 years ago. Decorate the invitation with pictures of the food. Maybe you could start with 'Fingers of smoked fish served on boiled seal flipper'!

CHIEFTAIN CHALLENGE

Imagine you were made the chieftain of fifty Skara Brae villagers. Whatever you say will be the law of the village. What five laws would you have for your people? Write them down.

Now imagine you are chieftain of your class at school. You are even chief over the head teacher and the classroom teachers!

What five laws would you make them obey now you are in charge? Write them down.

TOWN PLANNER

You have been shipwrecked on a desert island. It is as empty as Skara Brae once was... but warmer. There are plenty of trees to cut down, and a lot of tools have been washed ashore with you. You have walked around the island – so now draw a map of it.

On your trip, you found there are animals you can hunt, fish you can catch and fruits you can eat. There are even stones you can use for building – but you need to plan a small town for the thirty people who landed with you.

Add the town to your map. Think of all the things the people will need, to survive. The next ship to pass this way will not arrive for a year. Can you keep the people safe and happy with your plan?

Should there be a place where they can all meet? A square in the middle, perhaps? And should there be a statue carved and stood in the middle? A statue of you, of course!